PUFFIN BOOKS

The Day Matt Sold Great-grandma

leanor Allen was born in South
orkshire. She has written several
ildren's books, both fiction and non-
tion, and was inspired to write this story
ter looking at many old photographs of
r family. She is married with two
enage children and lives in Worcester.

ne Cope worked in publishing before
coming a freelance editor and travelling
ot. During this time she started drawing
d has now illustrated a variety of books,
m technical reference books to story
oks and cartoons. She lives in Devon
d is married with a young son.

CHILLERS

The Blob Tessa Potter and Peter Cottrill
Clive and the Missing Finger Sarah Garland
The Dinner Lady Tessa Potter and Karen Donelly
Ghost from the Sea Eleanor Allen and Leanne Franson
Hide and Shriek! Paul Dowling
Jimmy Woods and the Big Bad Wolf Mick Gowar and
  Barry Wilkinson
Madam Sizzers Sarah Garland
The Real Porky Philips Mark Haddon
Sarah Scarer Sally Christie and Claudio Muñoz
Spooked Philip Wooderson and Jane Cope
Wilf and the Black Hole Hiawyn Oram and
  Dee Shulman

CHILLERS

The Day Matt Sold Great-grandma

Eleanor Allen
Illustrated by
Jane Cope

PUFFIN BOOKS

PUFFIN BOOKS

Published by the Penguin Group
Penguin Books Ltd, 27 Wrights Lane, London W8 5TZ, England
Penguin Books USA Inc., 375 Hudson Street, New York, New York
10014, USA
Penguin Books Australia Ltd, Ringwood, Victoria, Australia
Penguin Books Canada Ltd, 10 Alcorn Avenue, Toronto, Ontario,
Canada M4V 3B2
Penguin Books (NZ) Ltd, 182–190 Wairau Road, Auckland 10, New
Zealand

Penguin Books Ltd, Registered Offices:
Harmondsworth, Middlesex, England

First published by A & C Black (Publishers) Ltd 1994
Published in Puffin Books 1995
10 9 8 7 6 5

Made and printed in Great Britain by William Clowes Ltd, Beccles
and London

Chapter One

One grey, dismal day, Matt trudged into town behind his mum. He had a problem. Tomorrow was Mum's birthday and he had to buy her a present.

He curled his fingers anxiously round the odd assortment of coins in his anorak pocket. It felt like a lot, but he knew that it only added up to eleven pence. Christmas had emptied his money-box a month ago and Mum couldn't afford much pocket money since Dad had gone away. He'd thought about borrowing from his big sister Jane, but decided against it. Last time he'd borrowed a measly fifty pence, she'd made him clean her school shoes for a week!

Matt still owes 25p!

Eleven pence. He jangled the coins in his hand. What could he buy his mum for that? He didn't think she'd appreciate a packet of bubble gum . . .

As they neared the Post Office at the bottom of Albert Road, Matt saw a neighbour, Mrs Graham, approaching. Mrs Graham was a gossip. She could cram more words into her mouth at once than anyone else Matt knew.

rhubarb, rhubarb, r
rhubarb, rhubarb, rhu
rhubarb, rhubarb, rh
rhubarb, rhubarb, rh

BORING!

He gave Mum's arm a warning tug, but she took no notice. She stopped and deliberately settled into her boots for a good chin-wag. Matt realised he was in for five minutes of kicking his heels – at least.

He tightened his scarf and glanced
around, wondering how to kill the time.

Next door to the Post Office was a junk
shop he liked, called 'Wotsits'. He decided
to wander over and take a look in there.

The dingy window was crammed with stuff. He ran his eye over a pair of carved wooden candlesticks; an old camera; some blue and white plates and a little glass dish. He thought the glass dish would look nice on his mother's dressing table. But it cost sixty pence.

Matt shuffled round to look in the side window. There was a handwritten notice sellotaped there. An arrow pointed downwards to a pile of brown-coloured photographs. Propped up on top of the pile was a photo of a lady dressed in old-fashioned clothes. The notice said:

SHORT OF CASH?

WHY NOT SELL GREAT-GRANDMA? GOOD PRICES PAID FOR VERY OLD PHOTOS LIKE THESE.

Matt was interested. He'd seen photos like that before. There were some at home in an old cardboard box in the attic. Gran had stored them there when she'd moved into her new retirement flat.

Some of those photos were of *his* great-grandma. He knew because one day Mum had found him looking through them and explained who all the strange-looking people were.

There were photos of great-uncles and great-cousins and all sorts of other relations, too. But great-grandmas seemed to be the ones in demand.

"Good prices paid . . ." thought Matt.

I'll tell Mum
—maybe Gran
could sell hers
to 'Wotsits'
and make some
money!

Matt turned to tell his Mum, but he didn't stand a chance. Words were still shooting out of Mrs Graham's mouth like machine gun bullets.

As he waited for Mrs Graham to draw breath, Matt had a brainwave.

What if he went up to the attic, took one of Gran's photos and sold it himself? Nobody would miss just one. They were only gathering dust.

His eyes slid over to the little glass dish. It would make a lovely present for his mum.

"What a great idea!" he thought.

Why don't I sell them MY great-grandma and buy that dish?

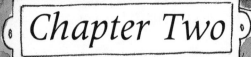

Chapter Two

That afternoon, while his
mum was busy hoovering,
Matt slipped up to the attic.
He found Gran's photo box
and sorted through the photos.
No doubt about it, he decided –
that was the one. It was the only
one of great-grandma on her own.

12

She was sitting on a spindly chair in front of some painted scenery and was all dressed up in a long dress with sparkly bits on the front.

What a cross patch!

Matt muttered, as he peered down at her thin face with its tight, narrow lips and hard eyes. Mum had told him that this fierce-looking lady had whacked Gran on the bottom with a carpet beater when she was a girl. Just for answering back.

He felt a shiver run down his spine.

"I'm glad she's dead!" he muttered. "I wouldn't fancy being whacked with a carpet beater!"

Determinedly he picked up the photo and zipped it inside his anorak.

Just going to my friend's house, Mum!

Then he ran to 'Wotsits' as fast as he could.

The man at the counter asked no awkward questions. He liked the photo and offered Matt fifty pence for it straight away. That was just right. Matt added another ten pence from his pocket and left the shop carrying the little glass dish wrapped in a brown paper bag.

That night, before he went to sleep, Matt went over to his chest of drawers and quietly pulled one open. He lifted up a sweater and took out the glass dish. He tried it on top of the chest, moving it around and admiring the way it shone under the electric light.

Mum would love it! And for only sixty pence it was a real bargain. Certainly worth more than a silly old photo!

Matt put the dish away again and climbed into bed. He was soon sound asleep. But in his sleep, strange things began to happen.

First he stirred restlessly. Then he began to toss around as though somebody had put itching powder in the sheets.

Suddenly he shot bolt upright.

Ouch! Ouch!

His eyes flickered open. He stared wildly round the shadowy room. He had dreamed that somebody had been poking him hard in the small of his back, then pinching him with really vicious pinches. "I must have been having a nightmare!" he thought. He lay back on his pillow and closed his eyes again.

Get me out of Alf Blenkinsop's window!

a voice grated, close to his ear. It was such a scary, menacing voice, it made Matt's flesh creep.

Oh no! I'm still dreaming!

Get me out of Alf Blenkinsop's window double quick you little good-for-nothing. Or—mark my words—you've not heard the last of this!

Who – who's there?

Matt sat up and stared around his dark, silent room. His scalp was prickling and all his hair was standing on end.

No one answered him. No one was there. The only sound he could hear was his teeth chattering.

Chapter Three

Next morning over breakfast Mum
opened the birthday card Matt had made
for her and the expensive one Jane had
bought. She was saving her presents until
teatime because this was the first day
back to school after the holiday and they
were all in a bit of a rush.

"Are you feeling all right?" she
asked Matt suddenly.
"You look a bit peaky."

"My tummy feels
queer," he said.
"But I think
I'll be all right."

It wasn't just his tummy that felt queer, it was all of him. But he didn't want to tell his mum. He was sure it had something to do with the nightmare. Somehow he felt as though it was still with him, lurking. Waiting to start up again. All that awful prodding and pinching. And the voice. That terrible voice, going on and on about somebody he'd never even heard of. Blenkinsop! What a stupid name!

Who's Alf Blenkinsop Mum?

Mum shrugged, "Never heard of him".

"I don't think we'd be likely to forget anybody with a name like that!" laughed Mum.

So where had the name come from?

Matt puzzled over it as he walked to school. It didn't seem like the sort of name he could have invented.
It seemed . . .

"Aaargh. . . !" he cried, for suddenly he slipped off the edge of the kerb, lost his balance and crashed down on to his knees in the gutter.

As he scrambled to his feet, Matt glowered angrily around. Because he was sure that slip was no accident. He'd been pushed!

There wasn't a soul in sight. No one who could have pushed him. And no one who could have been laughing the high-pitched laugh that seemed to be echoing in his ears.

It was just like the nightmare.

Chapter Four

When he got home, Gran had come to tea and soon Mum was cutting her birthday cake. Everything seemed so warm and friendly, Matt forgot to expect bad things.

When Mum began opening her presents from Jane and Gran, Matt ran upstairs to get the glass dish.

Happy birth-day Mum!

He proudly carried it to her in the paper bag.

Mum was just holding out her hands to receive it when

CRASH!

She told Matt he must have tripped over the edge of the rug. But he knew better. He knew he'd been deliberately tripped up again, by that invisible foot.

The glass dish in its brown paper bag shot out of his hand and bounced against the edge of the hearth.

Mum helped Matt up. Then she picked up the bag and peered inside. "Oh, no — what an awful shame!"

Such a pretty dish too Matt . . . Maybe we can superglue it.

She pulled out two separate chunks of glass and tried to slot them together.

"Where did you get that?" Jane asked.

"From 'Wotsits'," he said. Then added, "It was a bargain."

"What's 'Wotsits'?" asked Gran.

"A junk shop," said Jane. "At the bottom of Albert Road, by the Post Office."

I know it. Used to be Carter's Corner. And before that, going back to when I was a girl, it was Blenkinsop's— the pawnbroker's.

"Whose?" cried Matt.

"Alf Blenkinsop," said Gran. "Had it for years and years."

"Well that answers your question, Matt," said Mum. "You must have seen the name written somewhere when you went in to buy the dish."

"What's a pawnbroker's?" Matt asked, with a worried frown.

"A pop shop, we used to call them," said Gran. "Where folk went when they were short of cash. You took them something – say, a bit of jewellery or an ornament – and you left it with them. They lent you the money in exchange. When you could afford to, you bought it back again. They charged a bit extra for the service ... .

31

"Husbands' best suits . . ." continued Gran, who loved to talk about the past. "Folk pawned those in the bad old days. Even the kids' shoes; just about everything you can think of, bar the kitchen sink!

Made a lot of money out of other people's misfortunes," she added, "did Alf Blenkinsop. And the tale was, he wanted my mother to marry him. But she turned him down flat. Thought he wasn't respectable enough. Always too proud to step inside his shop, though all the neighbours used him. She'd have starved, and us kids with her, rather than go in there. . . ."

As Gran rambled on, Matt felt the blood drain out of his face.

Cold shivers ran through him, as though somebody was dropping ice-cubes down his back.

"Was – was that m-my great-granny?" he asked, just to be sure.

Gran nodded. "So keen on respectability was your great-grandma, Matt, that if she saw some of the things that go on these days – she'd turn in her grave!"

She's done more than that! Matt thought. I'm being haunted, by a great-grandma with a grudge! His throat grew so tight, the words would hardly come out.

"Did she h-hate Alf Blenkinsop?"

"Didn't hate him, so much as scorn him,"
said Gran. "Wouldn't have been seen
dead in his place . . ."

Matt swallowed hard. Worse and worse!

Great-grandma *could* be seen dead in Alf
Blenkinsop's place, right now! And it was
his fault. He'd put her there. For the sake
of a measly fifty pence.

"Are you still not feeling well, Matt?"
asked Mum, running an anxious eye over
him. "You look as if you've seen a ghost."

35

"You do that," said Mum.

Matt hastily pulled on his anorak and shut the front door behind him. It was a very dark evening and Mum wouldn't approve of his going all the way down to Albert Road on his own. He didn't fancy it much himself. But he had to know.

Chapter Five

'Wotsits' was shut. The shop was in darkness, but its windows were lit up by a nearby lamp. As he skidded to a halt by the side window, Matt's eyes filled with horror.

There sat his great-grandma, stiff-backed in all her finery beneath the arrow, propped up by an old cracked jug.

Matt had thought she looked grim before. Now she looked fit to murder somebody – him!

"I'm sorry!" he groaned silently. "Just hang on till tomorrow and I'll get you out. Cubs' Honour, I will!"

"You'd darn well better, you thieving little rascal!" snarled the angry voice in his ear.

And to show that she really meant
business, Great-grandma accompanied
her words with hefty, stinging blows to
his backside that felt as though they were
dealt by a carpet beater.

"Sixty pence?" said Jane next morning. "You must be joking!"

I need sixty pence — in a hurry!

Jane's eyes narrowed on him. "Why?"

"If you must know, I borrowed sixty pee off – off somebody – to buy that present for Mum. And now he wants it back, sooner than I expected. Like today."

You shouldn't borrow money, you know that. What would Mum say? Anyway I haven't got sixty p. Not till I've done that babysitting for Mrs Graham. You'll have to wait.

Matt ground his teeth. There was no one else he could ask.

Can I have it first thing tomorrow?

If you promise to work for it.

OK. What?

You'll have to wait and see.

Matt groaned in anticipation. But whatever Jane lined up for him, it would be worth it to buy back Great-grandma.

As he'd expected, Jane made Matt work hard for the promised loan. He did her share of the washing-up and mucked out her rabbit. There was an errand to run tomorrow.

The only good thing about the day, he thought, was that Great-grandma had left him alone . . .

Chapter Six

She'd just been biding her time, waiting till he was in bed!

Sixty peas!
You handed over
my photo for
sixty peas?

If she hadn't looked so terrifying, Matt might have wanted to laugh. But she had actually put in an appearance tonight. She was bending over his bed in her best black frock with the glittery bits on the front, and her eyes were glowing like coals. Her bony, prodding fingers, one with an old-fashioned, red-stoned ring, hovered menacingly close to his throat.

43

"*Pence*," Matt winced. "I sold it for fifty pence. I need sixty to buy it back."

"Sixty pennies?" Great-grandma only knew old money. She only knew pounds, shillings and pence. "Can't you raise five shillings?"

"I already told you, not till tomorrow."

Matt had been reminding himself all day that he'd never heard of anybody actually being killed by a ghost. Terrified out of their wits, maybe. But never killed stone dead. He decided to stand up for himself.

An ugly rattling noise came from the back of Great-grandma's throat. Her body shook with rage.

"Get it back!" she screamed, "Back into that box tomorrow – or I'll – " Her face contorted into an ugly grimace as she picked out the most dreadful punishment she could think of.

I'll set the house on fire!

The bony fingers snapped beneath Matt's nose and Great-grandma disappeared. But the menacing feeling and the nasty smell of her remained long after.

Matt knew she had meant it.

Chapter Seven

Late the following morning (which was Saturday) Jane at last gave Matt the sixty pence.

He ran to 'Wotsits' as fast as he could. He dived for the counter, money at the ready.

Can I buy my photo back?

Sorry, son.

"What?"

The man looked kind, but he was shaking his head very firmly.
"'Fraid you can't buy your photo back, because it ain't 'ere."

Matt's mouth fell open. Without a word he shot through the door and stared at the side window.

It was true – Great-grandma had gone!

Sold it more than an hour ago. A nice young chap. Seemed to know a lot about old photos.

That night Matt lay awake, guilty and tense. He was waiting for the smell of burning to fill his nostrils. He wondered if he should have warned Mum and Jane, but he didn't think they would have believed him anyway.

All night he lay awake and alert. Yes, *all* night – for suddenly daylight was filtering into the room. He couldn't believe it – it was morning and nothing had happened.

The house hadn't burned down around his ears. His body hadn't been prodded, pinched or punched.

Strangest of all, when he sat up he had
the feeling that Great-grandma was no
longer anywhere around.

Matt was amazed. Had Great-grandma
done her worst? Was setting fire to
people's houses more than a ghost could
do? Somehow Matt doubted it. There had
to be some other explanation. But if there
was, he couldn't come up with it.

Chapter Eight

A week passed by. Then two, and still nothing had happened. Gradually, Matt stopped puzzling over why Great-grandma had almost faded from his mind completely. So it came as a very big shock to feel that she was suddenly back again. He was on a school outing to the local museum, when it happened.

The class was passing through some rooms full of displays of old costumes. Matt stopped suddenly. He felt his scalp prickling, and she was definitely back in his head again.

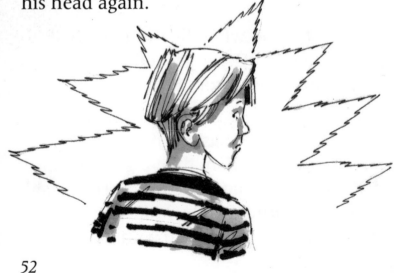

He glanced around nervously.

One large glass case had been furnished to look like an old fashioned parlour. Now he saw that the models in it were wearing dresses like the one Great-grandma wore. He felt himself being drawn towards them.

His mouth fell open in amazement. For there, standing on a little table in the display, was Great-grandma's photo in an elaborate silver frame. There she sat on her spindly chair, as proud and starchy as ever, yet different, somehow. It was a second or two before he realised what was different about her. It was her mouth. She wasn't exactly smiling, but somehow, almost.

Great-grandma was looking almost happy! Matt found himself smiling. Could it be that she actually enjoyed being on display in that big glass case? Well, it was certainly an improvement on Alf Blenkinsop's window.

I'll bet that's why she didn't bother to burn the house down. That man who bought the photo must have been from the museum. I think she's actually proud to be part of a museum display.

Matt felt very relieved that things had turned out so well for Great-grandma. But by the time he was on the coach going home, he found that he was starting to feel a bit anxious.

He knew his Gran enjoyed visiting museums and old houses. What if she should come to the museum, see the photograph and recognize it? She'd want to know how it got there. What a scene there'd be! Would they be able to trace it back to him?

Chapter Nine

For a day or two Matt worried about what to do. In the end he felt so bad about the whole thing, he decided he'd better tell someone.

The next time Gran came to tea, they went for a walk in the park together and he forced himself to tell her the whole story. He thought it sounded a bit stupid in parts, but Gran let him finish before she said anything.

"That's a really strange story, Matt," she said, thoughtfully. "I bet you think I'm going to shout at you for taking the photo, don't you?" Matt nodded.

"Well I'm not. It seems to me you've punished yourself enough already. Because I think that's what this is all about – a guilty conscience. Do you know what I mean?"

None of it really happened, Matt. Just a guilty conscience.

Matt shook his head.

I think you imagined your Great-grandma and all the nasty things that happened. And that was because deep down you felt guilty about taking the photo without asking. She never rose up out of her grave to haunt you. It was just your vivid imagination.

Matt was thoughtful for a moment or two. He was glad Gran wasn't cross with him. And he wanted to believe she was right and that he'd imagined it all. But . . .

59

"Do you really think so?" he asked doubtfully.

"Of course I do," said Gran. "And all's well that ends well," she added, bracingly. "I don't mind the museum having the photo. In fact, I'll send them some more, if they like. So just put it out of your mind, Matt. Forget it – I know I shall!

"Let's be getting home, it's turning chilly and I'm ready for a cup of tea."

As she spoke, Gran placed her hand comfortingly on Matt's shoulder.

On her finger flashed a large ring with a dark red stone.

Matt felt as though his insides had suddenly turned right over.

"That's not your ring, is it?" he mumbled.

"Yes it is," said Gran, touching it. "My mother left it to me in her will. But I don't wear it often. It's a bit old-fashioned.

I don't expect you've seen it before.

Gran blinked. For a moment or two she and Matt just stared uncomfortably at each other. It wasn't like Gran to be at a loss for words.

"There's always a simple explanation, Matt, for everything," she said at last. "I'll admit I can't think of one for the ring right now, not on the spur of the moment. But I expect one will come to me.'

"I expect so," Matt muttered.

But he was pretty sure there really was no explanation – and that Gran knew it too.

Some other Puffin Chillers

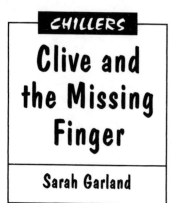

CHILLERS

Clive and the Missing Finger

Sarah Garland

What has happened to Clive's strange neighbour, the man with the missing finger? Why has he mysteriously disappeared? And what is his guilty secret?

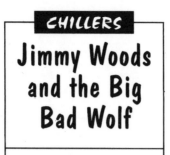

CHILLERS

Jimmy Woods and the Big Bad Wolf

Mick Gowar
Illustrated by
Barry Wilkinson

Jimmy Woods is the worst sort of bully, the sort that likes hurting people. But there is one thing he's really scared of and he's about to get the fright of his life!

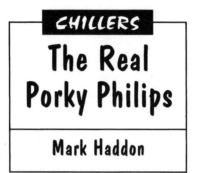

CHILLERS
The Real Porky Philips

Mark Haddon

Porky Philips is a boy whom no one really
notices. Even his family can't tell the difference
between him and the mysterious double who
threatens to take his place . . .

Coming soon in Puffin Chillers

CHILLERS

The Blob

Tessa Potter
Illustrated by
Peter Cottrill

The first blob appeared on Graham's book after second break. It was a rusty red colour and it looked suspiciously like blood.

Where did the sinister blobs come from? And did they have something to do with the locked classroom upstairs, or the strange new headteacher?

CHILLERS
Spooked

Philip Wooderson
Illustrated by
Jane Cope

The note said 'Please help me', and with it was a
dusty old photograph of a pale-looking girl. Pete
tried to forget them. Then he saw the face at the
window of the empty house. The same girl's face.
Who was she? Pete had to find out, and that
meant going into the house. Alone.

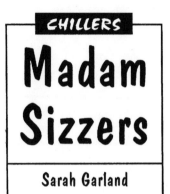

CHILLERS

Madam Sizzers

Sarah Garland

There's something creepy about Madam Sizzers.
Perhaps it's just her sharp red fingernails and her
gleaming scissors. Rachel and Lola try to annoy
her, but then they stumble upon a dark secret. . .